Emily's Dream

ORCA BOOK PUBLISHERS

National Library of Canada Cataloguing in Publication Data:
Pearce, Jacqueline, 1962-
Emily's dream / Jacqueline Pearce.

(Orca young readers)
ISBN 1-55143-368-0

1. Carr, Emily, 1871-1945--Childhood and youth--Juvenile fiction.
I. Title. II. Series.

PS8581.E26E45 2005   jC813'.6   C2005-901173-4

First Published in the United States 2005

Library of Congress Control Number: 2005922213

Summary: Young Emily Carr is determined to become an artist no matter what her big sister thinks about it.

Free teachers' guide available. www.orcabook.com

Orca Book Publishers gratefully acknowledges the support for its publishing programs provided by the following agencies: the Government of Canada through the Book Publishing Industry Development Program (BPIDP), the Canada Council for the Arts, and the British Columbia Arts Council.

Typesetting and cover design by Lynn O'Rourke
Cover & interior illustrations by Renné Benoit

In Canada:
Orca Book Publishers
Box 5626 Stn.B
Victoria, BC Canada
V8R 6S4

In the United States:
Orca Book Publishers
PO Box 468
Custer, WA USA
98240-0468

07 06 05 04 • 6 5 4 3 2 1

Printed and bound in Canada.

For my nieces and nephews:
Bailey, Tabitha, Jasmine,
Jordan, Brendan, Nicholas,
Aidan, Adam, Eric and Drew.
Believe in yourself
and stay true to your dreams.

Table of Contents

❧ 1 ☙
The Riding Whip

Emily burrowed into the sweet-smelling hay. She didn't think her oldest sister would climb up to the barn loft to look for her, but if she did, Emily would be well hidden. The stiff hay shafts poked into her, and the dust tickled her nose, but Emily didn't care. She could hear Dede's angry voice calling her from the house. Emily shifted deeper into the hay. She had no intention of going back to the house to let Dede punish her. She'd rather stay in the hayloft all day.

Why did Dede have to make such a fuss over everything? Emily was sure she'd seen Bishop Cridge hide a smile when she'd chased her little brother Richard into the sitting room and tagged him right over the tea things Dede had just set out for her guests. If Bishop Cridge hadn't minded a little tea in his lap, why should Dede? Dede had gotten bossier than ever since their parents had died.

It was three years now since Mother's death from illness, and Emily still missed her terribly. Father had seemed to lose interest in life after Mother died, and he hadn't lasted much longer. Now, Emily's grown-up sister Dede was in charge. Father had left the house to Dede, and Dede acted like she owned the Carr children as well as the house.

"She doesn't own me," Emily whispered fiercely into the hay.

"Emily Carr, you get in this house this minute!" Dede's order rang across the cow yard. "Or do you expect your brother to take your punishment for you?"

Emily sat up, hay cascading off her body. Through a hole between the boards in the side of the loft, she could see Dede standing on the back porch of the house. Richard—Dick, as everyone called him—stood beside

2

her, looking at his feet. Dede had a firm grip on his ear. Hay dust drifted up, and Emily sneezed.

Well, that was it. She'd have to go in. She couldn't leave Dick to take the punishment on his own. Playing tag had been Emily's idea, after all. Dede was so unfair.

Emily climbed slowly down the ladder from the loft. The family's old cow lingered by the barn door, waiting for her. Emily gave her an affectionate scratch on the head, then took a deep breath, squared her shoulders and headed for the house.

Once Emily was on the porch, Dede let go of Dick's ear and grabbed Emily's instead.

"You are so exasperating, Emily!" Dede said angrily. "When will you learn to obey the rules of this house?"

Dede pushed Emily through the back door into the kitchen, not expecting an answer.

"You will have our guests believing that we are uncivilized, that we have no sense of decorum or propriety," she went on.

Emily felt her own anger rise. Dede was always going on about what other people thought. She didn't care what Emily thought or even what Dick or Emily's other sisters thought. All that mattered to Dede was that everything looked right to others.

"You know the punishment for breaking rules," Dede said grimly as she reached for the riding whip that hung on the wall by the kitchen door.

Emily glared at Dede. She wanted to say something angry back at her, but instead she gritted her teeth and braced herself for the snap of the whip against the back of her legs.

Whack! *Whack*!

"And one more for hiding," Dede added.

Whack!

Then she let go of Emily and hung the whip back on its hook.

"I'm sorry to have to do that, Emily," Dede said. But Emily turned away from her. She did not want Dede to see the tears in her eyes.

"Can I go now?" Emily asked, trying to keep the anger and humiliation out of her voice. She did not want another smack with the whip.

"*May* I go," Dede corrected.

"May I go now?" Emily repeated, though she felt her face growing hot with resentment and frustration.

"Yes, you may," Dede said at last.

Emily walked slowly out of the room and along the hall to the stairs leading up to her bedroom. She wanted to stomp up the stairs, but she made herself walk quietly.

Once inside her room, Emily flung herself onto her bed and screamed into the pillow.

"Milly?" a timid voice whispered. "Are you okay?"

Emily rolled over and saw Dick standing by the door, pale and concerned. He looked younger than his years even though his yellow curls had been cut off, and he had recently started wearing long pants like a man.

"Of course I'm okay," Emily told him with a forced smile.

She got off the bed and stood beside the metal birdcage that hung on a stand near the window. Inside, the yellow canary cocked his head sideways to look at her, then opened his beak to let out a cascade of sound. Emily smiled—this time, for real. The canary's singing always improved her spirits.

Dick came to stand beside her.

"I'm sorry you got in trouble," he said. Then he looked at her with a mischievous twinkle in his blue eyes.

"But the game was fun," he said. "And the look on Bishop Cridge's face sure was funny."

Emily reached over and hugged her brother, laughing.

～ 2 ～
Daydreaming

On Monday morning, Emily and Dick walked to school with their sisters, Alice and Lizzie.

Dick, who was named after their father Richard Carr, was twelve, three years younger than Emily. Alice and Lizzie were two and four years older. Lizzie was already finished school, but she often walked with the others, then continued on to visit missionary friends, or their older sister Tallie, who lived in town. Between Lizzie and Emily's two older sisters, Tallie and Dede, there was a big gap in their family where two brothers had died as infants.

Tallie had left home to marry a naval officer and had children of her own now. Dede, the eldest, was fifteen years older than Emily. She had not married but instead focused her life on taking care of her family and doing Christian work. Both Dede and Tallie were proud to tell people they had lived in England before their parents moved to the colony town of Victoria.

As Emily and her brother and sisters left their house behind and headed down Carr Street toward the school, Emily and Dick slowed to let Alice and Lizzie get ahead of them. Emily noticed that Dick seemed withdrawn and pale. Ever since he was a baby, he had often been sick and tended to tire easily. He was generally a quiet boy, but there was a hidden spark in him that Emily enjoyed fanning to life. He could use some brightening up now, she thought, looking at him sideways.

Impulsively, she jumped off the wooden sidewalk onto the road and sprang back again. She knew she was being silly, but sometimes silly was the best thing. She bounced back and forth from sidewalk to road until Dick began to laugh, and she was out of breath.

"Emily!"

Up ahead, Lizzie and Alice had stopped and turned back. Lizzie scowled, her hands on her hips. Alice looked worried.

"Why can't you behave more like a lady—or at least act your age?" Lizzie said. "You are going to be dirty before you get to school."

"You're going to fall and hurt yourself," Alice warned.

"You are going to make us all late," Lizzie added.

Emily rolled her eyes at Dick.

"Yes, yes," she called to Lizzie and Alice. "We're coming, mother hens."

"Come on," she said to Dick, and she began to cluck and flap her elbows as she hurried forward. Dick hesitated for a moment, then he flapped after her, trying to keep his flaps a little more dignified.

Alice laughed as Emily and Dick caught up to her, but Lizzie turned her back on them and marched forward. Emily marched like a soldier, swinging her arms and lifting her knees high. Dick grinned and swung his arms along with her.

"Oh don't, you two," Alice whispered.

Lizzie's head snapped around, and Emily and Dick quickly slowed to a regular walk.

Emily glanced at Dick. His cheeks were pink again, and his eyes were twinkling. Emily felt better.

Once she was stuck in the school classroom, Emily's mood drooped. It was hard to pay attention to the dull lessons. Her eyes kept drifting to the windows. She could see trees outside and glimpse the road. A delivery boy rode by on a brown horse, balancing a basket on one hip. She watched him pass, envious. She would much rather be sitting on a horse than sitting at a desk. How wonderful it would be to throw her leg across a horse and shout "Giddyup!" as she often saw the butcher and the baker delivery boys do.

Emily remembered how she'd once dreamed of being a circus horse rider. She pictured herself in a fancy costume standing on the back of a white horse, her arms raised, people cheering.

Bang! The teacher's ruler slammed down on the desk top in front of Emily. Emily jumped.

"Miss Carr," the teacher said with exaggerated politeness. "I do wish you would give me the courtesy of your attention."

"Yes, sir," Emily said, sitting up straight and meeting the teacher's eyes in what she hoped was a contrite and polite way. Inside, her heart was thumping from the scare. She wished she were a good student like Alice and Dick. They always got good marks and never got in trouble for daydreaming. She could hardly wait until art class at the end of the week. At least then she would have no trouble paying attention.

"Now, let us see whether you can do the following sum," the teacher said as he walked back to the front of the class.

Emily sighed. She picked up a stick of chalk and prepared to copy numbers onto the slate board in front of her.

❧ 3 ❧

Art Class

After school on Friday, Emily walked on her own to the home of the art teacher, Miss Withrow.

Lizzie and Alice used to go to art lessons with her, but they did not have the interest in art that Emily did. They felt they had gone to lessons long enough.

"Once you have a husband and family to look after, you will have no time for art," Alice often reminded Emily.

Alice had been happy to take on more household duties since the death of their parents. She was always bustling around the house cooking or cleaning. Lizzie, on the other hand, always had her nose inside a

Bible when she was not scowling over chores or helping with church meetings. She was already congratulating herself on the missionary work she planned to do. Dabbling in art was a childhood trifle she thought best left behind.

For Emily, art was something else altogether. It was a physical thing that gripped her and would not let go. She could not stop herself from drawing just as she could not stop herself from breathing. It was part of her.

At Miss Withrow's, the art students sat at a long table laid out with paper, pencils and sticks of charcoal. Miss Withrow stood in front of them dressed like a schoolteacher with a white apron over her plain dark blue dress. Her brown mousy hair was pulled back from her face and sat at the back of her head in a neat fashionable bun. She handed each student a photograph over which she'd carefully stitched tiny squares.

"I want you to measure out the same number of squares on your large paper," she instructed the students. "You will then copy what you see in each small square on to your own corresponding large square."

Emily dove into the activity with enthusiasm, amazed as the small face in her photograph began to appear enlarged on her paper as she filled in the squares with detail. She glanced over at Sophie Pemberton, an older girl who sat across from her. Sophie leaned over her own paper, face intent. Like Emily, she too had a serious interest in art and a definite talent. Emily would have liked to talk with her about it, but Sophie seemed so much older and surer of herself. She was tall, slim and elegant, her glossy chestnut hair already pinned up into a mature style. Next to her, Emily felt clumsy and childish. Her own dark brown hair refused to stay tamed by its ribbon and hung in loose messy curls around her face.

Sophie noticed Emily looking at her and smiled. Emily smiled back, embarrassed but pleased. Although they hadn't said a word to each other, Emily felt a warm glow of satisfaction—as if, with the smile, she and Sophie had exchanged an understanding.

Emily returned to her drawing. Once again she was caught up in the thrill of the pencil moving on the paper, bringing an image to life under her hand.

After class Emily walked home along the wood planks at the side of the road. The center of the road was muddy and churned by horses' hooves. On the other side of the plank walkway ran a shallow ditch, and beyond that a tangle of wild roses grew, sweet with the scent of new leaves. The thought of spring's arrival made Emily's feet feel lighter as she skipped along the boardwalk. She paused on the James Bay Bridge to look down at the tide coming in over the mud below. No one was down at the water today except a few shore birds poking along the edge of the mud. When the tide was out, Indians from the Songhees Reserve often pulled their canoes up onto the mud flats. They dug for shellfish and searched for useable items in the heaps of garbage dumped down the hill by people in the city.

Dede did not approve of Emily lingering on the bridge or near the mud flats. Emily wrinkled her nose the way Dede did whenever she crossed the bridge, mimicking Dede's manner of sniffing the air with distaste. The fresh briny scent of the incoming tide was beginning to cover the stink of garbage and drying seaweed. Unlike Dede, Emily found the smells intriguing. But remembering Dede made Emily start walking again, hurrying her pace. She'd get another scolding if she were late getting home.

❦ 4 ❧
Guests

Once she was inside the house, Emily sensed right away that something was different.

Warm air greeted her as she shut the front door behind her. Normally, the house was almost as chilly as outside, with a fire lit only in the small sitting room near the kitchen. Warmth in the front drawing room and dining room meant there were guests. Emily could hear voices she didn't recognize coming from behind the partially closed drawing-room door, but she couldn't see inside. A man's new black coat and bowler hat hung in the hallway next to a stylish royal blue woman's cape. These were not Dede's ordinary churchy visitors.

"Emily, is that you?" Dede's voice called from the drawing room. "Come in and say hello to our guests."

Emily glanced down at the coat she still wore. It was tolerably clean. If she kept it on, Dede would not see the charcoal and ink that streaked her white pinafore. She took a breath and stepped into the drawing room, pushing the door open in front of her.

Dede sat in a straight-backed chair by the side window, needlework resting in her lap. On the plush rounded chairs on either side of the fireplace sat a man and a woman Emily didn't recognize.

Dede gave Emily a disapproving look, and Emily remembered too late that her hair had come loose from its ribbon.

"Emily," Dede said, keeping her voice pleasant. "This is Mr. and Mrs. Piddington from England. They'll be staying with us for awhile."

"Pleased to meet you," Emily said, giving them the polite smile and small curtsy Dede expected.

"What a charming young girl," said the woman, who held a white lace handkerchief near her thin pinched-looking face as if she expected she might need to protect her nose from a bad smell at any moment. Her eyes flicked to her husband's with a look that suggested her real opinion of Emily was the opposite of her words.

"Indeed," the man said, giving Emily only a glance. His dark hair was combed slickly to one side, and he had a long face exaggerated by long sideburns. He reached for a cookie from a plate on the small table beside him and poked the top one aside as if he thought a better one might be hiding behind it. Then he took his hand away, looking down his long nose as if none of the cookies met with his approval.

"This is the Piddingtons' first visit to our city," Dede went on as though she had not noticed Mr. Piddington's rudeness.

"Yes," Mrs. Piddington said with her phony smile. "Your city is even smaller and more charming than I expected."

Her words sounded like a compliment, but

they felt more like an insult to Emily. What Mrs. Piddington really seemed to be saying was that she thought Victoria was much too small and insignificant. Emily suspected that "charming" was a word Mrs. Piddington used for anything she thought unsophisticated and inferior. The answering look in Mr. Piddington's eyes seemed to agree.

"I hope you will excuse me for a few minutes," Dede said as she got up from her chair, setting her needlework aside. "I must attend to the supper."

"Emily," she added. "Go upstairs and change, then come down and see if our guests need anything."

Emily followed Dede out the door. She made as if to head right up the stairs but turned back once Dede had disappeared into the kitchen. She pressed her ear to the drawing room door.

"You'd think they'd have at least one house servant," Mr. Piddington's nasal voice said with a note of disgust.

"Imagine dear Dede and the younger sisters having to prepare all the meals themselves."

Mrs. Piddington's voice dripped with phony sympathy. "It must be such a lot of work looking after a house without servants." She said the word "work" with distaste.

"There is little else to occupy them here, I am sure," Mr. Piddington pointed out, sounding bored.

A chair creaked as if one of them might be getting up, and Emily pulled away from the door. Quickly, she walked up the stairs, keeping her feet quiet. Her hands were balled into angry fists at her sides. She definitely did not like the Piddingtons.

∝ 5 ∝

Not Like London

"Do you always dine this early?" Mr. Pidding-ton asked, sitting at one end of the long dining room table. He did not sit up straight but stuck his long legs out to one side and leaned back in his chair as if he were loung-ing. It seemed disrespectful to Emily—as if he did not think their dining room worthy of his whole attention or manners. She resent-ed that he had been given Father's old place at the table.

"In London, one never sits down to supper before nine or ten," explained Mrs. Piddington as she delicately arranged her napkin on her lap.

"This isn't London," Emily snapped. Dede gave her a warning look across the table.

"Of that, we are very much aware," drawled Mr. Piddington.

"May I interest you in some roast, Mr. Piddington?" Alice interjected, standing to serve him. Alice was always the peacemaker.

"I've taken the liberty of hiring a cab for tomorrow," Dede said, changing the subject. "I thought you might enjoy a turn around Beacon Hill Park and a drive along the ocean. Some spring flowers should be in bloom now."

"Aren't you a dear," Mrs. Piddington said, her voice oversweet. "I'm sure that would be lovely."

Emily turned to Dick, who sat beside her, and held her napkin up to her face so that only he could see her gagging expression. He laughed, and Dede gave the two of them a quick, suspicious look.

"I need a cab for tonight as well," Mr. Piddington announced. "Seeing as how we'll be finished eating so early, I might as well go out."

"Oh." Alice looked flustered, but Dede was calm as ever.

"I'm afraid we don't have a horse of our own, and it's too late to order a cab now," she explained.

"Too late?" Mr. Piddington sounded as if he didn't believe Dede. "But it's not even seven."

Emily thought she detected a flicker of annoyance cross Dede's face, but Dede hesitated for only a moment.

"I could send Emily and Dick into town," she said.

"Oh, that's right," Mr. Piddington said. "I'd forgotten you have no servants."

"Yes," Dede said, her voice thin. "We thought it best to manage on our own after our father's death."

"Idle hands are free for the devil's work," Lizzie put in, as if this explained everything.

"You'll find this is a modest home, Mr. Piddington," Dede continued. "I apologize if it is not what you are accustomed to, but we find it suits us well."

"And we do appreciate your hospitality," Mrs. Piddington said loudly. "I was just saying to Mr. Piddington how charming your home is and how delighted we are in your company."

Emily met Dick's eyes. He too seemed to see through Mrs. Piddington's false compliments.

After dinner was over, Dede insisted that Emily and Dick be sent to hire a cab for Mr. Piddington. Mr. Piddington offered no objection despite his wife's assurances that the Carr's "charming quiet lifestyle" was just what the two of them needed at the moment and that they hated to put anyone to any extra work.

Emily and Dick walked along the darkening road toward town, glad to be out of the house and away from the guests, but resentful at being sent on an errand for Mr. Piddington.

"How *charming* you simple and dull Victorians are." Emily mimicked Mrs. Piddington's shrill honeyed voice, waving her hand as though she held one of Mrs. Piddington's lace handkerchiefs.

"Yes, your dull quiet lifestyle suits us fine," Dick said, deepening his voice to imitate Mr. Piddington. "But send me a servant! Send me a cab! Lick my boots!"

Emily broke into laughter, staggering against Dick for a moment. Dick tried to keep his head up so he could continue looking down his nose at her the way Mr. Piddington did, but he was overcome by giggles and bent over, clutching his stomach. Finally, their laughter died away.

"Enough of those horrible Piddingtons!" Emily said. "Come on, I'll race you to the bridge."

Their feet drummed along the boardwalk as they ran, heading for the lights of the town and the livery stables.

❧ 6 ❧
Another Arrival

Emily put clean water and birdseed in her canary's cage, whistling softly to him at the same time. She closed the cage door and sat back on her bed. The bird began to sing. At first he whistled back at Emily, then his notes expanded into a beautiful trilling song. He sang as if he was truly happy, and Emily felt cheered. She'd always wanted an animal of her own. Ever since she was little she'd wished for a dog, but Father, and now Dede, would not allow a dog in the house or in the garden. She'd saved her own pocket money to buy the canary, and she loved him dearly. But, the past few days she'd been feeling sorry for the bird stuck in his cage.

Since the Piddingtons' arrival she had felt like a bird in a cage herself, and she hated it. She had to tiptoe around the house on her best behavior.

"Stand up straight. Walk more slowly. Fix your hair ribbon," Dede would whisper whenever Emily passed her. There was nowhere to escape to because she never knew where Mr. and Mrs. Piddington or one of Dede's regular churchy guests would turn up. Even in the garden or cow yard she would find someone glaring at her with disapproval, and the smell of Mr. Piddington's nasty cigarettes seemed to follow her everywhere. If only she could get away on her own.

Midweek, Emily came home from school to find another change. The horse barn was no longer empty. Emily ran to the fence to admire the new occupant. An old dark bay horse stood placidly in the field beside the barn, looking as comfortable as if he'd always lived there. He ambled toward Emily, nostrils testing the air for her scent. She bent down and plucked a handful of the long sweet grass that grew beside the fenceposts.

"Hello there," Emily said, holding the grass out to the horse. He leaned toward her and took the grass in his lips, pulling it into his mouth and crunching it with long yellow teeth.

Emily held her hand against the horse's muzzle, letting him smell her. She was amazed at his muzzle's velvety softness. The horse's black whiskers tickled her hand, and warm air blew from his nostrils. She reached up to stroke the coarse hair of his nose, and he pushed against her hand to show that he liked her touch.

"I'm pleased to meet you too," Emily said.

The horse looked at her steadily with large brown gentle eyes.

He was wonderful.

Rattling and banging at the barn door interrupted Emily's pleasure in the horse's company.

"Emily!" Dede called from the barn. "Help me get the horse harnessed to the phaeton." Dede was pulling the small carriage out from the barn, bumping it against one of the doors as she did so.

Emily hurried through the gate and up to the barn to help Dede. Together, they tugged the carriage out through the double doors. Then Dede brought the halter over to the horse.

"What's his name?" Emily asked. "Where did you get him?"

"Just a minute, Emily," Dede snapped as she struggled to pull the halter over the horse's head. The horse ducked his head helpfully and stood still.

"There," Dede said as the halter slipped into place. She led the horse over to the carriage, and Emily hurried along beside her.

"I bought him from Mr. Mitchell," Dede said at last. "He's got a few years left in him, and he's a good all-around workhorse. He's well behaved, and Mr. Mitchell said he'll carry a rider or pull a carriage."

"And his name?" Emily prompted.

"He's called Johnny," Dede said as she harnessed the horse to the carriage.

"Johnny," Emily whispered, bending close to the horse's nose so that she could feel his

warm breath on her face. It felt like a secret or a promise shared between them.

"Can I go for a drive?" Emily asked as Dede climbed up to the carriage seat, holding her skirts in one hand.

"Certainly not," Dede said. "Mr. Piddington is taking the carriage. I'm just bringing it out to the front of the house."

Emily's heart sank. The arrival of the horse had made her forget about the Piddingtons. But now they dropped back in front of her like a big stone in her way. Her disappointment over not getting a ride in the carriage turned to anger as she realized that Dede had purchased the horse just to please Mr. Piddington.

"Why can't he buy his own horse?" Emily said.

"Emily!" Dede said warningly. "The Piddington's are our guests. They are guests to our city and to our home, and I intend to show them the best hospitality possible. Furthermore, I did not purchase the horse for Mr. Piddington. I wanted the use of the phaeton myself to visit house-bound church members."

When the Carrs had last had a horse Dede had often taken old people out for drives or visited sick people on the edge of town, but Emily was sure Dede was just using this as an excuse now. However, she kept this thought to herself and stepped back from the carriage as Dede took up the reins and gave them a shake. Johnny started to walk, and the carriage moved forward.

"Open the gate!" Dede ordered, and Emily ran ahead of Johnny to throw open the double fence gate. She glared after the carriage as it drove through, then she shut the gate and latched it. She watched the back of the carriage until it disappeared around the front of the house.

At least Mr. Piddington would be away from the house for awhile.

～ 7 ～
Serving the Piddingtons

Supper was late because Dede made them all wait for Mr. Piddington's return. At last they heard the carriage pull up in front of the house and Mr. Piddington come in the front door.

"He's just left the horse there," Emily complained. "Does he think servants are going to come dashing out to do everything for him?"

Dede's eyes narrowed.

"You and Dick go," she ordered. "And make sure you put the carriage away properly."

"I won't be his servant!" Emily protested.

"Don't be selfish," Dede said. "Do you want the horse left standing?"

Mrs. Piddington's shrill voice carried down the hall as she greeted her husband. Emily turned back to Dede.

"I'm only doing it for the horse," she hissed and hurried away before she had to see Mr. Piddington. Dick followed her as she slipped out the back door.

Johnny was still breathing heavily when Emily and Dick reached him, his sides heaving in and out.

"That nasty Piddington better not have worked you too hard," Emily whispered to Johnny.

"Yeah," Dick said, coming up beside her. "I bet he stayed too long at one of the road-houses and then had to rush back."

They walked Johnny over to the barn and unhitched him from the carriage.

"I heard he used to be a circus horse," Dick told Emily. "Do you think it's true?"

Emily shrugged. She remembered the day several years ago when a circus had appeared in the field across the street. It was before the new houses had been built. She'd gone to bed one night, and the next morning three big, striped tents had been poking up into the sky. She hadn't even heard the wagons arrive or the tents being set up. Father had taken them all to see the animals and the big top show, and Emily had watched with envy the fancy-dressed woman who rode a horse around the ring, standing on its back.

Emily walked Johnny around the field until he had cooled down and his breathing was regular. As she led him back to the barn, he nudged her gently with his nose, and she scratched the top of his head. It was hard to imagine this quiet old beast galloping around a circus ring.

Back at the barn, Dick had found a piece of old blanket to rub the sweat and road dirt from Johnny's body.

"There you go, Johnny," Emily said as they finished. She stroked the horse's neck, and he whickered softly. Emily didn't care whether or not he really had been a circus horse. It was enough that he was here.

Inside the house, Emily and Dick cleaned up and hurried into the dining room. As

Emily passed Mr. Piddington, she was sure she smelled liquor on him. She wondered if Dede knew where her precious guest had spent his time. Dede did not approve of roadhouses and taverns.

After supper, Dede and the Piddingtons retired to the drawing room, while Emily and her other sisters cleared the table and washed the dishes. Although Emily had always helped with the cleaning up after supper, it felt different with the Piddingtons staying at the house.

"They think we're servants," Emily said to Alice.

"Don't be silly, Emily," Alice said. "Do you expect guests to wash their own dishes?"

"I bet neither of them has done a speck of work in their whole lives," Emily said.

"Let he who has never sinned throw the first stone," said Lizzie.

Emily groaned. "What's that supposed to mean?"

"It means, you only talk to try to get out of doing the work yourself," Lizzie said.

"That's not true!" Emily's voice rose.

"Hush!" Alice whispered.

Emily turned her back on Lizzie and thrust her hands into the soapy sink water, attacking the dirty dishes.

"Not so hard!" Alice urged. "You're going to break a dish."

Once the dishes were done, Emily retreated upstairs to the room she shared with Alice.

"I wish you could be more patient, Milly," Alice said softy, following Emily into the room. "The Piddingtons won't be here much longer."

"Oh, have they said when they're planning to leave?"

"No, but..."

"Doesn't Dede see through them?" Emily asked, not letting Alice finish.

"See through what?" asked Alice.

Emily looked at her.

"Oh, never mind," she said. She knew Alice was reluctant to believe anything bad of anyone.

Alice was quiet for a minute as she let down her long red-brown hair.

"Don't you see, Milly?" she said after awhile. "The Piddingtons' visit is good for Dede."

Emily sniffed.

"You want her to have friends, don't you?" Alice continued. "You don't want her whole life to be just taking care of us."

"I guess not," Emily said, feeling a bit guilty. Still, she didn't know what Dede saw in the Piddingtons.

❧ 8 ☙
A Proposal

The next day, Emily came home from school to find Johnny in his field and the Piddingtons nowhere to be seen.

"They've gone out in a hired dog cart," Dede told Emily. Emily knew this was a high two-wheeled cart that men liked to drive.

"Is our horse and carriage not good enough for them?" Emily fumed.

A dark look crossed Dede's face. Emily wondered if it was only her words that had annoyed Dede or if Dede might actually be offended by her guests' actions.

"We have to excuse men," Dede said lightly. "They'd rather sit up high and look out over everything than ride in a low women's carriage."

Men. Why did they get to do whatever they wanted?

"You can't blame anyone for wanting the best view along our ocean drive," continued Dede.

Emily doubted the Piddingtons knew how to appreciate any view properly, but she didn't say this out loud. Her mind returned to Johnny. He wouldn't be getting any exercise today. If only Dede would let her ride him.

Emily opened her mouth to ask, then caught herself. If she blurted out the idea, Dede would surely say "no" on reflex. Emily would have to broach the subject a little more carefully.

"Are you going to be taking the carriage out later?" Emily asked.

"No, not tonight, Emily."

"Has the horse had any exercise today?"

"No."

"Will you be taking him out tomorrow?"

"I don't know, Emily," Dede snapped. "If

you're wanting me to take you for a drive, I don't have time to take the carriage out just for fun."

"I know," Emily said carefully. "I was just worried about the horse not getting enough exercise."

Dede looked troubled.

"Yes, I thought the Piddingtons would be using him more," she said, more to herself than to Emily. "And I've got the bishop coming over tomorrow, so I won't be able to go anywhere."

"I could ride him around the back field," Emily suggested, trying not to let her eagerness show. "Just to give him a bit of exercise."

"Hmm." Dede sounded doubtful. "I don't know if you could manage him, Emily."

"I've ridden at the Cranes', and I know how to take care of a horse," Emily said. The words came out in too much of a rush, and Dede narrowed her eyes. Emily took a deep breath and tried to sound practical.

"It's a job Alice and Lizzie won't want, and you said yourself how busy you are."

Dede sighed. "Yes, I suppose it's the only thing to do when I won't be able to take the carriage out myself."

She looked thoughtful.

"But the back field is too full of holes. You'll have to ride on the road."

Emily's heart leapt. This was even better than she'd hoped. She nodded, afraid that if she spoke she might say something to change Dede's mind.

"You are old enough," Dede said, though she did not sound convinced of this. Emily thought of all the times she'd gotten in trouble lately and been accused of not acting her age.

"You will have to keep to the nearby roads," Dede added. "I don't want you riding through town or going too far."

"Yes, Dede," Emily said, composing her face into what she hoped was an obedient and trustworthy expression. "I could take him out now and be back in time to set the table for supper."

"All right," Dede said. "I'll watch how you ride out of the driveway."

Emily headed to the back door, careful not to hurry. She could hardly believe her luck.

"Emily!" Dede's voice sounded stern, and Emily froze, one hand on the doorknob. Had Dede changed her mind already?

"You must ride like a lady," Dede told her.

"Yes, Dede," Emily said. She pushed open the door and was out of the house, a grin of triumph wide across her face.

～ 9 ～
Johnny

Out by the barn, Emily called Johnny, and he trotted over to her. She wished she'd thought to bring him a carrot from the pantry, but all she had to offer him was another handful of long grass. She used it to coax him into the barn. The old sidesaddle and bridle hung on the wall beside his stall. Emily wondered for a moment if she could get away without using the saddle, but Dede would be watching her, and Dede had said she had to ride like a lady. Ladies did not ride like men or boys with their legs spread over a horse's back. Ladies rode sidesaddle with both legs on one side of a horse, well covered by a long skirt.

Emily dusted off the saddle and placed it on Johnny's back, fixing the girth strap under him. Then she slipped the bridle over Johnny's head and buckled it securely. She stood back and looked the horse over, frowning at the saddle. When she'd ridden a horse at the home of their family friends, the Cranes, she'd been young enough to ride cross-saddle and had not had to worry about her dress hiking up and her legs showing. But now Emily was almost grown up.

Emily had watched the oldest Crane girl ride sidesaddle. The girl had talked with an air of superiority about how it was done, showing off her skill, and Emily was sure she could remember everything she needed to know. But first, she had to get on the horse. At the Cranes', they'd always had help mounting their horses.

Emily looked around the barn for something she could stand on. She found an old wooden box and dragged it over to Johnny's side. She took hold of the reins with her right hand and stepped onto the box, trying to remember how she'd seen the Crane girl place her body as she was helped up to the saddle. The girl had held onto the pummel with her rein hand, and Emily did the same. She took a deep breath and jumped up. She made it part way, then slid back down the horse's side.

"Drat!"

Steadying herself, Emily tried again. This time, she landed in the saddle and quickly placed her left foot in the stirrup and hooked her right knee over the pummel. Then, with some difficulty, she adjusted her tangled skirt. She shifted the reins to both hands and called out with satisfaction.

"Giddyup!"

Johnny walked forward, and Emily found herself facing the same direction as her legs, off to the left. How could she ride like this? She remembered what the Crane girl had said about keeping her right shoulder back and looking straight ahead between the horse's ears. She shifted her balance accordingly, and by the time she and Johnny rode out past the front of the house where

Dede stood watching from the porch, Emily felt confident she would pass Dede's inspection. She smiled and waved.

"Wait!" Dede called.

Worried, Emily glanced down at herself. No, her legs weren't showing. Her skirt was hanging properly.

Dede came down the front steps, holding something out to Emily. It was the riding whip—the same one Dede had used on the back of Emily's legs more than once.

"You'll need this," Dede said.

Emily took the whip and waited for Dede to say more. But Dede stepped back.

"Well, go on then," she said with a nod toward the road. "Don't be too long."

Emily took up the reins again and urged Johnny forward.

"Let's go," she told him softly.

Johnny walked at a steady sedate pace down the driveway, and Emily concentrated on sitting straight and square in the saddle, holding the reins just right. Once they had turned on to the road and were out of Dede's sight, Emily relaxed.

"Come on, Johnny!" she called out. "Let's have some fun!"

She pressed her left leg into Johnny's side and tapped his other side with the whip. Johnny shifted to an eager trot, and Emily began bouncing up and down in the saddle, her hair shaking loose from its ribbon. After a few jarring moments, she caught the horse's rhythm and began to move more comfortably. Soon they were riding down the quiet lane through Beacon Hill Park, and Emily slowed Johnny to a walk again.

The whole park was alive with growing. On both sides of the road, the dark green branches of cedar and fir trees hung like graceful skirts, their edges trimmed with pale new green. Maple trees unfurled tender new leaves, and the pale white blossoms of wild cherry trees glowed in the shadows. Sweet smells filled the air.

Johnny seemed to know his way, so Emily relaxed her hold on the reins and let herself drink in the beauty around her.

❧ 10 ❧
Serious Art

"I don't want to see any outlines," Miss Withrow told the art class as she walked around the room. "In nature, there are no lines around objects."

Emily looked down at her paper and rubbed at a dark line with her finger. She looked up at the bowl of fruit they were all supposed to be sketching. Miss Withrow had arranged apples and pears in a shallow blue bowl in the center of the long art table. Emily had sketched their rough shapes on her paper and was beginning to fill them in with different tones of her pencil, pressing harder for the dark shadows and receding areas. She looked back to her paper and decided the smudging she'd just done created a nice modeled effect, giving her apple more roundness.

"Miss Withrow?"

Emily turned to see Sophie Pemberton with her hand raised and her eyes looking to the art teacher with suppressed excitement.

"I have some news," Sophie continued when Miss Withrow acknowledged her. "My parents have agreed that I should go to England to study art. They've written to the Slade School of Art in London, and I've been accepted."

A buzz of excitement rose around the room.

"Congratulations, Sophie!" Miss Withrow said, smiling and clapping her hands together. "How wonderful for you."

Emily looked at Sophie with envy and awe. She was so lucky. Everyone knew that if you wished to be a serious artist you'd have to go abroad to study. There were no art schools in Victoria yet or even in Vancouver, the nearest large city. The best schools were in London, England or Paris, France—both very far away. Dede would never let Emily go away to study. The idea of leaving home and leaving Victoria was a scary thought as well. Sophie must be very brave and confident. Even if her mother went with her, Sophie would need a lot of courage to study among strangers in a place that might not take a girl from Canada seriously.

"There you go, girls," Miss Withrow said, looking over her students. "Perhaps our Sophie will inspire others among you." Her eyes rested briefly on Emily. Emily looked away. Miss Withrow couldn't be suggesting that she, Emily, should go to art school. Emily did love art, but she was sure she didn't have nearly enough talent or courage.

After breakfast the next day, Emily stole back up to her room. It was Saturday, so there was no school. She slipped a sprig of groundsel weed she'd found near the front of the house into the canary cage and whistled a greeting to the bird. The cage stood in front of the dormer window next to her easel. She'd made the easel several years ago, using branches Father had pruned from the big cherry tree at the side of the house.

That was when she'd first felt the urge to be an artist. She'd tried more than once to put the urge aside and concentrate on being more like what her family wanted her to be, but it was never any use. Art always pushed its way back. She couldn't ignore her need to draw and create, but to go away to art school? That was something she didn't know if she'd ever be ready for.

Emily looked out the window into the branches of white blossoms. Perhaps she could sketch one of the branches. But where was her sketchbook? She looked around the room and didn't see it. Thinking back, she remembered having it with her in the sitting room after school yesterday. She must have left it there.

Emily raced down the stairs. In the hall, she could smell the vile smoke of Mr. Piddington's cigarettes. Voices came from the sitting room, and Emily hesitated outside the door.

"She does draw rather prettily," said Mrs. Piddington's voice. It was less shrill than usual, but there was still something about it that Emily disliked.

"If you say so," Mr. Piddington answered, sounding bored as always. "I suppose they're not bad for an annoying kid."

Suspicion set Emily's heart pounding. She stepped into the room to see Mr. and Mrs. Piddington sitting with her sketchbook between them, flipping the pages. Mrs. Piddington looked up, startled, but Mr. Piddington only glanced at her.

Outrage and disbelief coursed through Emily.

"How dare you look through my private book!" she shouted, striding up to them and snatching the book from Mrs. Piddington's hands.

"Well, isn't she touchy?" Mr. Piddington said with a trace of amusement. He sucked deeply on a long brown cigarette and blew the smoke in Emily's direction.

Emily waved the smoke away with her book, her eyes sparking with anger.

"You—" She pointed a finger at Mr. Piddington, ready to tell him what she thought of him.

"Emily!" Dede's sharp voice came from behind Emily, stopping her words.

"I hope my sister isn't being rude," Dede said to the Piddingtons.

"They had my sketchbook," Emily told her.

"Emily, please don't interrupt me." Dede kept her voice pleasant in front of the Piddingtons, but Emily could hear its dangerous undertone.

Mrs. Piddington waved her handkerchief.

"We were just admiring her sketches," she said sweetly. "We meant no harm."

"Yes, quite," Mr. Piddington said, agreeing with his wife. "The kid just overreacted."

"I'm not a kid!" Emily cut in angrily. "And you have no right to look through other people's things."

She thought she saw Mr. Piddington smile slightly, as if he'd been expecting her reaction. At the same time, Dede took hold of her elbow in a pinching grip.

"Apologize to our guests, Emily," Dede ordered quietly.

Emily clamped her mouth shut and glared at the Piddingtons. She realized that, for the first time, Mr. Piddington did not look so bored, and she wondered if he was enjoying seeing her in trouble. She watched him take another long drag of his cigarette. This time, when he exhaled, he blew the smoke carefully off to the side of the room.

"Emily, I said apologize to our guests."

Emily heard the threat in Dede's voice, and she was sure the Piddington's did too. If she did not apologize she would be whipped again. She remembered all too well the sting of the riding whip on the back of her legs. But still, Emily said nothing.

"Very well, Emily. You give me no choice." Dede's grip on Emily's elbow tightened further as she directed Emily out of the room. As Emily turned, she thought she saw the corners of Mr. Piddington's mouth twitch into a smile.

Emily hardened herself as Dede marched her to the kitchen where the riding whip hung. She would not make a sound, and she would not cry, Emily told herself.

She gritted her teeth against the first blow.

↜ 11 ↝
Revenge

The tears came later as Emily saddled Johnny and buried her face in his warm neck. Everyone seemed to be against her. If only Mother were alive. She at least would sympathize with Emily. Even if she didn't understand Emily, she would not be so hard on her. And if Mother and Father were still alive, the horrible Piddingtons wouldn't be staying with them.

Emily put her arms around Johnny's neck, breathing in his comforting animal smell. He blew softly, standing patiently as she held him. Emily took a deep breath and wiped away her tears. She would get back at Mr. Piddington somehow.

Once they were away from houses and people, Emily loosened the reins and let Johnny take the lead. They passed farmers' fields and tangled hedges of wild roses. When they came alongside a thick forest, Johnny suddenly veered toward it, heading right for the trees. Alarmed, Emily moved to tighten the reins and turn Johnny back to the road. But then she saw the path. The trees parted, and Johnny took them in.

He walked calmly along the trail. The trees seemed to close in behind them, and Emily had to duck her head under low branches more than once. Here and there, fingers of sunlight reached down into the forest, touching leaves, stroking tree limbs. The leaves rustled softly, the sunlight shifted and danced, and Emily felt her anger and frustration ease away.

After a while, the trail opened into a small clearing. Johnny stopped in the middle of the open space, and Emily slid off his back. She left Johnny to graze and sat down under a tall oak tree, leaning back against the firm solid trunk and closing her eyes.

Around her, the leaves whispered, and she felt the warm touch of sunlight on her face—gentle as her mother's hand. Her own hand rested on a rough cool root, and she sensed the slow movement of sap under the bark, like the pulse of blood through her own body. She opened her eyes, and green light dazzled her. All around her was the green movement of life. It coursed through the trees, through the birds, through the tiny insects crawling and flying, through the new sprouts and leaves, through the trunk she leaned against, and through her. For a wonderful dizzy moment, she did not know where she stopped and the forest started. She was part of it all, and it was part of her.

As the feeling began to slip away, Emily grasped after it. If only she could paint the forest as she felt it — capture this moment in paint and color so she could keep it with her. Emily blinked and sighed. She'd once heard real painters visiting from England say it couldn't be done. They said the British Columbia forest was too wild and untamed to paint. But they didn't know the forest like she did. Maybe there was some way to paint it—to paint how it felt today.

Emily stood up, suddenly frustrated. She didn't know enough about art. She had to learn more. But there was no one in Victoria who could teach her what she wanted to know. Across the clearing, Johnny blew and tossed his head. Emily glanced up at the sun and put the thought of art lessons out of her mind. It was time to get back.

Dick met Emily at the barn.

"Are you okay?" he asked.

Emily's thoughts were still full of the forest, and she smiled.

"Don't worry," she said. "Johnny and I rode away Dede and the Piddingtons."

Dick grinned.

"I wish I could do that," he said. "I've got to hide up in my room pretending to feel sick or overwhelmed with homework to escape them."

He helped Emily put away the bridle and saddle and rub down Johnny. They left

Johnny grazing contentedly and headed to the house. Emily's stomach grumbled. She'd been away so long she'd missed lunch. She expected Dede to greet her with more angry words, but the house was quiet.

"Don't worry," Dick whispered. "They've gone out."

Emily glanced cautiously into the drawing room.

"Are you sure?" she asked. She could see Mr. Piddington's silver cigarette case lying on the table between the two stuffed chairs.

"Yes. They hired a chaise to go visit a naval friend at the base in Esquimalt. Dede went too. They'll be away until evening."

Relief washed over Emily. What luxury to have the whole house to themselves!

"Where are Alice and Lizzie?" she asked.

"In the kitchen cleaning up," Dick said. "Alice saved you some dinner."

"Good," Emily said, still caught in the drawing room doorway. Instead of heading to the kitchen, she stepped into the drawing room. Dick followed her.

"What are you doing?" he asked.

Emily wasn't sure. Her feet seemed to have a will of their own. She stopped in front of the little table and put one finger to her lips to hush Dick. Then she snatched up the silver cigarette case and pushed it deep into the pocket of her pinafore. Dick's eyes widened.

Later that evening, Emily heard the chaise drive up. She listened from her room as Dede and the Piddingtons came through the front door and hung up their coats in the hall. She heard them moving about, then Mr. Piddington's voice calling to his wife.

"I thought I'd left it in the drawing room, but it's not there."

"Are you sure you didn't have it with you when we went out?" Mrs. Piddington asked.

"Of course I'm sure. I noticed the case was missing as soon as I went to get a cigarette." Mr. Piddington sounded annoyed.

Up in her room, Emily smiled to herself.

✥ 12 ✥
Unease

"You haven't seen Mr. Piddington's cigarette case, have you Emily?" Dede asked the next morning.

"No." Emily busied herself buttering a slice of bread and did not meet Dede's eyes.

After breakfast, Dede drove the Piddingtons to church in the phaeton, while Emily and the others walked. The morning was already warm, and the sun silvered the blades of grass as the four of them cut across the field behind the house. Emily and Dick dropped behind Alice and Lizzie.

"Dede asked me about Mr. Piddington's case," Dick told Emily in a whisper.

Emily glanced at Dick's face. He looked pale and worried.

"What did you tell her?"

"I said that I saw Mr. Piddington with it yesterday morning, which wasn't a lie," Dick said. He looked Emily in the eye. "I don't like lying—especially on a Sunday."

"Pah!" Emily said. "Sunday shmunday. You sound like Lizzie." She gave Dick a playful nudge. "Don't you think the horrible Piddington deserves it?"

Dick had to grin in agreement.

"Besides," Emily added. "I'm doing everyone a favor by hiding those stinky sticks."

She and Dick wrinkled their noses and laughed. But despite her careless words, Emily felt a worm of unease squirm in her stomach.

Dick's face grew serious again.

"If you get caught you'll be in real trouble," he said.

Emily couldn't help wincing at the thought of the riding whip nipping the back of her legs.

"It's not like I stole anything," she said quickly. "I'll just let Piddington stew a bit, then I'll leave the thing somewhere he can find it. He'll just think he misplaced it."

"What are you two whispering about?" Lizzie demanded. She had stopped and turned to glare back at them.

"Do catch up!" Alice pleaded. "We don't want to be late for church."

Emily rolled her eyes. Her pious sisters always started out so early Sunday mornings there was little chance of them being late no matter how much she and Dick dawdled.

The church service was long and dull, as usual. The minister, Dr. Reid, droned on and on, his thick white beard rising and falling almost hypnotically. One of the smaller orphans who sat near the church stove snored softly. Emily nudged Dick and pointed at an orphan boy who sat in front of them. His brown hair stuck up in ragged tufts on top his head, and he was holding a hymn book up to the boy next to him, using his body to hide it from the view of the matron who sat at the end of the row. Emily and Dick had a clear view of the book between the two boys. Scrawled in the margin was a childish drawing of Dr. Reid, his beard extra long with what looked like a bird poking its head out of the long flowing white mass. Sniffs of laughter escaped Dick and Emily, and Lizzie gave Emily a sharp poke.

Emily turned her attention back to the front of the church and tried to concentrate on Dr. Reid's words. With Emily's luck, Dede would probably quiz her on the sermon when they got home just like Father used to do. After a while Emily's attention wandered again, and she leaned forward to try to catch a glimpse of the Piddingtons who sat at the end of the Carrs' row. Mrs. Piddington faced straight ahead, her expression vacant. She was probably thinking that women's hats were much more stylish in England, Emily thought. Mr. Piddington looked bored, as usual. His heavy-lidded eyes seemed to be staring up at a corner of the ceiling behind Dr. Reid's head. Then, as Emily watched, he absently patted the empty pocket of his coat where his cigarette case usually rested, and his bored look hardened into a scowl. Suddenly, he turned, and his eyes met Emily's. She looked away quickly and drew back in the row. Her heart thudded. Did he suspect her of taking the case?

Eventually, the service ended, and Emily and her family emerged from the church, blinking in the sunlight. Dick caught Emily's eye as they watched the Piddingtons climb into the phaeton.

As they walked home, Emily watched the side of the road for signs of the weeds her canary liked to eat. She picked a few sprigs of a plant with small yellow flowers that Father had once told her was related to the dandelion. The thought of her canary pecking his food and singing made Emily's heart feel lighter.

~ 13 ~
Missionaries

Since no work was done on Sundays in the Carr house, the noon meal was the usual cold meat and dishes prepared the day before. The Piddingtons sat at the table while Emily helped her sisters bring in the food. As she set down a basket of buns, Emily noticed Mr. Piddington pick up the teacup in front of him and look at it with distaste. It was covered with wobbly hand-painted roses that had faded to an ugly brown color and had been a gift to Dede from one of her Sunday-school students. It wasn't usually used for guests and must have been set out by mistake.

"Good God, this is ugly," Mr. Piddington said, hardly making an effort to lower his voice. "It'll taint the taste of the drink."

Emily glared at Mr. Piddington, and Mrs. Piddington waved her handkerchief at him.

"My dear Mr. Piddington," his wife said. "I do think misplacing your cigarettes has put you out of sorts."

Mr. Piddington grunted in agreement.

"And no shops in this God-forsaken place are open on Sunday," he grumbled.

God-forsaken? Emily's temper rose. She had half a mind not to return his horrible cigarette case at all.

Just then, Mr. Piddington seemed to notice that Emily was in the room. Her face flamed as he looked at her. She turned away and hurried back out to the kitchen.

During the meal, Emily was careful to sit on the same side of the table as Mr. Piddington, so that he could not look at her directly. She did not like the way his eyes darted to her whenever the missing cigarettes were mentioned.

Soon after they'd finished eating, Emily was relieved to see the Piddingtons leave in a hired carriage. Unfortunately, they were replaced by two new visitors, missionary women with plain stern faces and dark unadorned dresses. Emily and Dick were forced to sit stiffly in the drawing room along with their sisters and their guests.

Teacups clinked softly, and women's voices droned. Dick rose from his chair.

"Excuse me, Dede," he said weakly. "Would you mind if I went to lie down for awhile?"

"Are you not feeling well?" Dede asked with concern.

Dick nodded, his eyes downcast.

"Yes, do go and lie down. I'm sure our guests will excuse you."

Emily looked anxiously at Dick. He had seemed so well earlier. Was he getting sick again? As he turned to leave the room, Dick winked at Emily. Relieved, she had to hold back a laugh. What a good idea. She wished for a moment that she hadn't always been so strong and healthy. Dede would never believe her if she tried the same rouse.

Once Dick had left, Emily sat back in her chair and sighed, resigning herself to a boring afternoon.

But the afternoon did not turn out to be boring, after all.

"The totem poles are heathenish," one of the missionaries was saying. "And the forests are so thick and wild you can't even walk in them."

Emily's ears pricked up.

"You've visited the Indian villages?" Emily asked, leaning forward in her chair.

"Why yes, dear. We just spent a year in a village on the north coast of Vancouver Island."

"How wonderful!" Emily exclaimed.

The missionary ladies looked pleased with Emily's interest, mistaking it for religious zeal. But Emily was remembering the exciting stories her father had told years ago after he and a group of local businessmen had hired a steamship to take them all the way around Vancouver Island. It had taken them ten days to get around the island. They'd passed mysterious Indian villages where tall poles carved with animals and supernatural figures stood. They'd seen whales and dolphins leaping in the water and had glimpsed bears and other wild animals at the edge of the forests. Her father had marveled at the magnificent trees, their closeness to each other, the strangling undergrowth and the great silence of the forests.

Once, when the boat was tied up for three hours, Emily's father and another man had tried to cut their way into the thick forest with axes. By the time the ship's whistle blew for them to return, they were exhausted and dripping with sweat, but they'd barely made a mark on the forest. These stories about the wild West Coast were much more interesting to Emily than the stories people told when they'd come back from a trip to England and Europe, bragging about all the great and important buildings and museums they'd seen. She longed to see the forests and the totem poles.

"What was it like?" Emily asked the missionaries eagerly.

"It was always wet," said the smaller of

the two women. "And there was nothing but fish to eat."

"It is difficult to live so isolated from Christian civilization," the taller missionary added. "But one can endure many hardships when one knows one is doing God's work."

Emily noticed that Lizzie was nodding her head vigorously as the guests spoke.

"But what about the forest and the people?" Emily asked.

"Oh, we never went into the forest," said the smaller missionary, sounding shocked at the suggestion. "It was much too dangerous."

"And we had no reason to," added the other.

Emily could think of many reasons why she would want to go into the forest—just to see what it was like, for one.

"The people must have been very grateful to have you bring them the word of God," Lizzie said.

"I don't know if grateful is the way I would describe their attitude," the tall missionary said. "But I believe we have made some headway in their acceptance of our Lord."

Emily turned away to hide her disgust. The missionaries were just as snobby as the Piddingtons. It seemed like they hadn't bothered to learn anything about the people or the place they had visited.

❧ 14 ❧
Poor Mr. Piddington

It wasn't until the missionary ladies were on their way out that Emily had a chance to slip Mr. Piddington's cigarette case under one of the stuffed chairs. She pushed it back far enough that it couldn't easily be seen. She doubted that Mr. Piddington had gotten down on his hands and knees to look under the chair already.

After supper, the Piddingtons had still not returned. It was so pleasant to have the house to themselves again—to be able to relax and not worry about tripping over the Piddingtons or any other guests—that Emily forgot about the case waiting under the drawing room chair.

Dick had made his way back downstairs. He, Emily and Alice sat reading in the sitting room, while Dede played hymns on the drawing room piano and Lizzie sang along. The music was sober and heavy as it vibrated through the house, but it was also familiar and comforting.

Feeling in good spirits, Emily put her book down suddenly and ran lightly up the stairs to her room. She came back down, carefully carrying the canary's cage. She placed it on the small table between her chair and the window and sat back down with her book. Both Alice and Dick looked up and smiled. It had been a while since Emily had brought the bird down to join them. Soon the canary's whistling voice was joining in with the piano, adding a more cheerful melody to the booming chords.

It was almost time for bed when Emily heard the carriage pull up in front of the house and the front door open. The memory of the Piddingtons and the cigarette case crashed down on her like a sour piano chord. She'd have to wait until they were out of the hallway before she could sneak past them and up to bed. She wanted to be far away when Mr. Piddington discovered the case under the chair.

The next morning it was obvious that the case had not yet been discovered. Mr. Piddington was making plans to head into town to buy more cigarettes as soon as the shops were open. How was Emily going to get him to find the case before he went out?

"Milly!" Alice called. "Are you ready to leave for school?"

Emily hesitated. It would be perfect if the case could be found while she was away at school. But how was she going to get someone to look for it?

Emily noticed Dede heading to the sitting room with the feather duster. Perfect. She would be making her way to the drawing room next. Maybe she'd find the case before Mr. Piddington left for the shops. But she'd be dusting the tops of things, not the bottoms. What if she didn't look under the chairs?

Emily grabbed her coat from its hook in the hallway outside the drawing room and paused in the drawing room doorway to put it on. Her eyes searched the room, unsure of what she was looking for. Then, she saw it—Dede's needlework. She glanced down the hall to make sure Dede was still out of sight and ducked into the drawing room. Carefully, she placed Dede's needlework on the floor as if it had fallen between the table and the nearby plush chair. She listened to make sure no one was coming, then she bent down and looked under the chair. The cigarette case was still there. She moved it slightly, so that it would be visible to anyone reaching down to pick up the needlework. Then she left the room and hurried to join the others leaving for school.

"You'll never guess," said Lizzie when Emily and the others arrived home after school. "Dede was dusting in the drawing room this morning, and what do you think she found?"

"What?" Emily asked, though her heart was pounding.

"Why, Mr. Piddington's cigarette case," Lizzie announced, sounding as pleased as if she had found it herself. "It was right under his feet all along."

Emily and Dick exchanged a quick look.

"Oh, I am glad for Mr. Piddington," Alice said. "He must be pleased it's been found."

"Yes," Lizzie said. "But he would have been more pleased if it had been found before he went out and bought another."

Emily felt a stab of guilt. But she was distracted when Dick suddenly pulled away from them and hurried up the stairs, clutching his stomach. Alice and Lizzie paid no attention, but Emily was concerned. Was he ill?

She caught up to him at the landing at the top of the stairs.

"Dick, are you all right?" she whispered, reaching out to touch his arm.

Dick turned to her, and as his eyes met hers, his face split into a laughing grin.

"Poor Mr. Piddington!" he whispered with a puffing exhalation of breath.

❦ 15 ❧
Close Call

The next day, Emily walked back to the house after another happy ride with Johnny. As she opened the side door, she caught a flash of something small and yellow moving through the air in the middle of the kitchen.

"Quick Emily, shut the door!" Alice cried. "Your canary is out."

Emily ducked into the kitchen and shut the door behind her. She looked around quickly and saw the canary flap against the window above the sink. Then, as Alice lunged toward him with her hands open, he flew up out of reach and back across the kitchen into the breakfast room.

"Stop chasing him," Emily commanded. "He'll never settle if he's scared."

Emily followed the bird into the breakfast room, trying to move calmly, so that she wouldn't frighten him further. Inside her chest, her heart was jumping. What if she had let the canary out when she opened the door to come in? What if he'd flown away and been lost?

"I'll close the door to the hall and get his cage," Emily told Alice. "If we can keep him in this room, and he calms down, he might just fly back into the cage."

Emily slipped out of the room, shutting the door behind her. She sprinted down the hall and started up the stairs to her bedroom. Dede stuck her head out of the drawing room.

"Slow down, Emily," she hissed.

Emily ignored her sister, hitched up her skirt and took the stairs two at a time. She skidded to a stop in the middle of the bedroom floor. Where was the birdcage?

Emily began to clatter back down the stairs, but Dede stood near the bottom of the stairs, hands on her hips, her mouth a thin angry line. Emily slowed.

"It's my canary," she told Dede, hoping Dede would understand the urgency of the situation. "He got out, and I'm trying to find his cage."

"The cage is in the sitting room," Dede said grimly. "Perhaps if you kept better track of where you left your creature in the first place, he wouldn't have gotten out."

Emily didn't bother to argue with Dede. She hurried to the sitting room and found the cage sitting on the table by the window. What did it matter where she left the bird, as long as he was in his cage and the cage door was shut? She always left the cage door closed securely. The only way the canary could have gotten out is if someone had opened the door when she was out riding Johnny.

Emily carried the cage to the breakfast room and knocked lightly on the door.

"Alice, it's me. Is it safe to open the door?"

The door opened a crack, and Alice waved Emily inside the room.

"He's sitting on top the cupboard," Alice whispered, pointing.

Emily set the cage down in the middle of the breakfast table and faced the open cage door toward the canary. Then she refilled the bird's water dish.

"I'll just go out quickly and pick some of his favorite weed, and then maybe we can lure him back to the cage," she told Alice.

It didn't take Emily long to find a sprig of the yellow flowering plant. She reentered the room cautiously and made her way back to the table. The bird was still sitting on top of the cupboard. He cocked his head sideways at her approach and began to preen his feathers.

Emily set the weed inside the cage and gestured for Alice to stay back. She whistled softly. The bird stopped his preening and looked up. He gave a tentative return twitter. Then he raised his wings and launched himself off the cupboard straight for the open cage door.

"Can we be of help?" The breakfast room door burst open, and Mr. Piddington's voice boomed into the small room. Mrs. Piddington followed him, leaving the door open wide behind her.

The startled canary changed direction midair, flew over the human heads, through the open door and into the hallway beyond. Mrs. Piddington screeched and waved her handkerchief above her hair.

"You did that on purpose!" Emily accused as she brushed by the grinning Mr. Piddington and followed the yellow blur of feathers into the hall.

"I'm sorry," Mr. Piddington said, sounding more amused than regretful. "I guess our timing was a bit off."

Emily rounded the corner just in time to see the canary veer away from the closed front door, turn sharply and sail up the stairs. Emily returned to the breakfast room and grabbed the cage.

"And stay out of the way!" she ordered the others as she rushed back out, but she kept the words under her breath, knowing Dede was near.

Sure enough, Dede appeared in the drawing room doorway as Emily hurried by.

"I said slow down, Emily," Dede warned. "It's just a canary, not a life or death emergency."

The canary had flown right into Emily's room, and once Emily was inside with the door shut and the room quiet, it did not take long for the bird to fly back into his safe and familiar cage. Soon he was pecking happily at his dinner.

Emily collapsed onto her bed, relieved and worn out. The canary was safe. But how had he gotten out? She remembered the smug look on Mr. Piddington's face after he and his wife had opened the door and let the bird fly out. She was sure he'd done it on purpose. Had he opened the cage door as well? Emily was sure he had.

❧ 16 ❧
Regatta

The next week was torture. Emily yearned to get away from the house—away from the stifling rules and phony politeness, away from Dede and the Piddingtons—but she was afraid to be away one minute more than she had to be. What if she went for a ride on Johnny and came back to find the canary cage empty?

Emily felt powerless. She couldn't say anything to Dede, and she was forced to be polite to the Piddingtons or risk getting into more trouble. If she told Dede she was worried that Mr. Piddington might let the canary out, Dede would only laugh and say Emily was being ridiculous and

90

self-important. She couldn't very well admit to Dede that she thought he might have let the canary out the first time to get back at her for the cigarettes going missing. Even worse, Piddington knew she was trapped, and he was enjoying it.

At supper, Emily exerted the tiny bit of power she had. When she set the table, she made sure to give Mr. Piddington the ugly hand-painted cup. She relished his look of distaste as he was forced to drink out of the cup. To complain about the dishes in front of Dede, his host, would have been too rude, even for him.

Emily confided her suspicions to Dick. He was outraged and sympathetic, and he chuckled when she told him about the teacup revenge.

"Don't worry," he told her. "I heard the Piddingtons say they were planning to leave for San Francisco after the Queen's birthday."

"At last!" Emily exclaimed.

"I'm glad they'll be gone before I leave," Dick added.

"What do you mean?" Emily asked.

"You know I'm starting school back East in September," Dick said.

Emily went cold. She'd forgotten the family plan to send Dick to a private school in Ontario. Mr. Lawson, the lawyer who was the children's legal guardian, was arranging it in keeping with their father's wishes. Now, it seemed, it was really going to happen.

"This house is going to be dull without you," Emily said.

"I don't leave for months yet," Dick reminded her. "Besides," he added. "We've got the regatta to think about now!"

Queen Victoria's birthday was on May twenty-fourth, and every year the city that was named after her celebrated with a wonderful regatta. When Emily was small, the family usually had a picnic in Medina Grove on the Queen's birthday, but once she and Dick were old enough to sit balanced in a boat, they went to the regatta at the Gorge.

The Gorge was an arm of the sea that ran from Victoria's inner harbor inland for three miles. The banks of the Gorge were still forested, but here and there, stately houses perched with gardens running down to the water. The water of the Gorge was warmer than the waters of the beaches around Victoria. Emily had sometimes been allowed to bathe in the ocean near Beacon Hill Park, but the nightdress she wore floated to the top of the water, leaving her legs bare and icy. It was difficult to swim in a dress, so she hadn't done much more than get wet, and she'd never learned to swim properly. At the regatta, people sat in boats, picnicked on the shore and watched the boat races.

On the morning of the Queen's birthday, Emily looked out her bedroom window. Rain had spattered the ground yesterday, but today the sun was out, and the air was sweet with the smell of hawthorn and other blossoms. There would be good weather for the regatta and for the first day of summer frocks.

Emily, Dick, Alice and Lizzie walked into town, while Dede and the Piddingtons followed in the phaeton. They joined with friends, Mr. and Mrs. Bales and their children, at the shipyard near the Point Ellice Bridge. The rosy-faced Mr. Bales helped everyone into rowboats, storing the picnic supplies in the boat with him and his wife. They pushed off and rowed under the Point Ellice Bridge that crossed the start of the Gorge waterway. Overhead, the bridge rumbled with the sound of traffic crossing on the way to the regatta. All along the arm, buggies and wagons stopped, horses were tied to bushes, and people made their way, laden with picnic baskets, down through the woods to the shore. Great strings of colorful pennants stretched out across the water from one side to the other, and the sound of band music grew louder as the boats made their way down the Gorge.

Emily clutched the side of the boat as it rocked in the water, feeling her stomach lurch. She was relieved when the small flotilla of rowboats nosed up against the shore. The men and boys jumped out first to help the ladies and deliver the picnic supplies safely to shore. The roar of the big naval guns fired at Esquimalt Harbor signaled the start of the regatta, and a bugle blown from the Gorge Bridge called the boats to assemble for the first race.

Both sides of the Gorge waterway were lined with people cheering and waving as the first naval boats cut their way down the middle of the arm, racing from the Gorge Bridge to Deadman's Island. As the boats rounded the island and headed back, the shouts from shore grew louder. One boat of uniformed navy officers had pulled into a clear lead. Emily and Dick struggled to see as onlookers crowded in on either side of them, pushing them back.

"I wish we were out on the water," Dick said, straining to see around a large woman with a huge white dress and matching parasol. "We'd have a better view."

At the edge of the water, they saw Mr. Piddington and some of the Bale children climbing into one of the rowboats.

"Come on!" Dick called, tugging on Emily's arm.

"Not with him!" Emily said, drawing back.

"It'll be okay," Dick said. "We can ignore him and just watch the boats."

The bugle sounded for the next racers to assemble. Emily caught a glimpse of the long slender dugout canoes coasting into place. The Indian canoe races were the most exciting of the regatta. Down on the water would definitely be the best place to watch.

"Oh, all right." Emily gave in and followed Dick.

Mr. Piddington gave them an uninviting look as they climbed into the boat. The bang of a gunshot signaled the start of the race, and nine canoes shot forward. Down the length of each long canoe, ten men dipped their paddles in one movement, while the steersman in the rear grunted out the rhythm. The sleek canoes seemed to fly over the water.

As the race finished, the wake of a small steam launch jockeying into the shore among the other watching boats set Emily and Dick's boat rocking. Emily's stomach churned, and she was sure her face was turning green. Mr. Piddington gave her an appraising look. His mouth twisted into a grin.

"Let's make the kid seasick," he called out.

He pulled in the oars, grabbed hold of the boat's sides and rocked. The youngest of the Bale children squealed with delight as the boat tipped back and forth.

Dick saw Emily's face.

"Hey!" he objected, but it was too late. Emily's stomach heaved. Clutching the side of the boat and fearing she might fall overboard, Emily leaned out over the water just in time.

~ 17 ~
The Whip Again

Emily shrank back into the boat. Dimly, she heard Mr. Piddington and the others laugh.

"That was a rotten thing to do," said Dick.

"It was just a bit of fun," Mr. Piddington declared. "If the kid can't take being on the water, she shouldn't have gotten in the boat."

Emily was too ill to do anything but slump against the side of the boat, holding onto her stomach, but under her fog of seasickness, her anger grew. How dare he make her sick? How dare he call her "the kid" as if she were a little child he could push around?

Once the boat was back on shore, Emily struggled out and collapsed onto the grass. Dick sat down beside her, while Piddington and the other children strode past them toward the picnic site, laughing.

Emily gulped air until the queasiness passed and the ground felt steady. Her anger rose up and boiled over. She pushed herself to her feet and marched after the others.

"Emily, wait!" Dick jumped up and called after her, but Emily did not stop.

"You!" she pointed, striding straight up to Mr. Piddington. "You made me sick on purpose!"

"Emily!" Dede cut in quickly. "That's no way to talk to a gentleman."

"He is no gentleman," Emily said, shaking with anger. "He is a lazy sponger and a cruel bully!"

Emily heard the sharp intakes of breath all round her. Even Dede's mouth dropped open.

"The kid has insulted me," Mr. Piddington sputtered.

Emily looked around at the shocked faces

and knew that this time she might have gone too far. Dede's face had darkened ominously.

"Emily, you must apologize to Mr. Piddington at once!" she ordered, making an effort to keep her voice quiet and controlled.

"I will not apologize for speaking the truth," Emily said, and she clamped her mouth shut tight. She was in for it now, but she didn't care. Enough was enough!

Dede's anger had not diminished by the time they all arrived home. She marched Emily straight to the kitchen and the riding whip.

"I've never been so embarrassed in my life!" Dede said through clenched teeth as she grabbed the whip from its hook. "Your behavior has shamed our whole family."

"But he—," Emily began, but Dede cut her off.

"I don't care what he did." She turned Emily away from her with one hand and raised the whip with the other. "You were not brought up to speak that way to your elders—let alone to a gentleman who is a guest in our home."

Swish! The whip bit into the back of Emily's legs. Emily sucked in a shocked breath at the strength Dede had used.

Smack! The whip snapped again.

Whack!

Emily began to feel faint, but stubborn anger kept her on her feet. Why couldn't Dede see how unfair she was being? Why couldn't she see what Mr. Piddington was like? Dede pretended affection to Emily in front of others, but she punished Emily for speaking the truth, for standing up to a cruel bully. It wasn't right.

Dede raised her arm for another swing. Emily braced herself, but as she did, she felt renewed outrage. This time, as the whip came down, Emily turned, reached out her arm and grabbed.

The whip stopped in midair.

"Enough!" Emily said, looking straight into her sister's eyes. "I am almost sixteen now, and if you thrash me ever again, I will strike back."

Dede glared at Emily, but Emily did not look away, and she did not loosen her grip on the whip. After a moment, Dede's hand let go, and the whip dropped to Emily's side.

"Very well," Dede said, her voice emotionless. "If you think you are too old to be disciplined, I will not whip you. But if that's the way you want it, then I expect you to act your age and start behaving like a young woman with responsibilities and duties, not like a child who has nothing in her head and does whatever she wishes."

✿ 18 ✿
The Sky Beckons

It was dark by the time Emily got to bed. She took a candle to light her way up the stairs and set it on the chest of drawers in her bedroom. Alice hadn't come up yet, and Emily stood in front of the chest looking into the mirror that hung above it. Beyond the reflected candlelight, dark eyes stared back at her. It was as if Emily was seeing herself for the first time. A young woman stared back at her, not a child—a young woman with a firm set to her round face and a spark in her dark eyes.

Today she had stood up to Dede. She had surprised herself with her own courage and determination. Now it seemed anything might be possible. But what did Dede mean when she said she expected Emily not to behave like a child? Emily knew all her sisters thought her art was child's play. Did Dede want Emily to give up art? Had Emily gained one thing only to lose another?

Emily stepped to the easel that stood in shadow by the window. She fingered the paper propped at the front of the easel, then picked up a paintbrush off the ledge. She turned the brush over in her hand, savoring the familiar weight and feel of the slim wood. No. She could not give up art.

The next day, the mood in the house was heavy. Mr. Piddington and Emily glared at each other, and Dede's eyes followed Emily with a dark critical look. Only late in the afternoon was Emily finally able to saddle Johnny and escape.

As she and Johnny left the yard, Emily could still feel the weight of everyone's expectations and criticisms on her shoulders, as well as a lingering pain in the back of her legs. But as Johnny carried her farther away from the house, the weight fell away.

In its place was a rising sense of marvel and pride at what she had done yesterday—she had stood up to both Mr. Piddington and Dede. Johnny's step, too, seemed to lighten the farther away they rode.

Finally, the houses and fields gave way to bushes and trees, and Johnny slowed, dropping his head now and again to nose the underbrush at the edge of the road. When he found a spot that seemed to satisfy him he parted the bushes with his head and took Emily through to a new trail. Emily felt a thrill of excitement as they left the road and the trees closed in behind them. The trees welcomed her into their midst. The branches brushed away all the lingering dust of what other people expected her to be. The forest embraced the pure Emily.

"Whoa, boy." Emily called Johnny to a halt as sudden inspiration filled her. She dropped off the horse and stood beside him in the tight space of the narrow trail. Then, she bent and undid the saddle girth strap. She lifted off the cumbersome side-saddle and placed it carefully out of sight in the bushes beside the trail, marking the spot in her mind. Then stepping up onto a handy tree stump to gain some height, she pulled herself up to Johnny's bare back and sprawled across him on her stomach.

"Just a minute, Johnny," she crooned softly as she swung her right leg over his back and shifted up to a sitting position. She hadn't managed it as smoothly as the butcher and the baker boys did, but she was up and riding cross-saddle. If Dede could see her like this, with her skirts hiked up and her stockings showing, she would be appalled.

"Come on, Johnny!" Emily called.

Johnny picked his way along the trail, which began to climb, and Emily adjusted herself to the new way of sitting. Suddenly the trees opened up. Johnny trotted out into a clearing at the top of a hill. Emily bounced on his back, her whole body facing forward. A new sense of freedom filled her.

At the crest of the hill, a twisted wind-blown arbutus tree gestured at the wide sky and the ocean beyond. Emily swung her leg off Johnny's back and slid to the ground. She loosened his bridle so he could nibble on the grass. Then she stood by the tree and drank in the view of sky and sea. It filled her up. She felt as if she were expanding— growing as huge as the sky. She loved this place—this whole wild West Coast. It was her home, perhaps even more than the Carr house was. But she knew now that she had the courage to leave it—not forever, just for a while. She, Emily, could do it. She could go and study art. She could learn what she needed to know to become a real artist and to paint the places that she loved.

~ 19 ~
Looking Ahead

In the weeks that followed, the Piddingtons left, summer arrived and Dick began to prepare to head to school back East. Again and again Emily tried to talk to Dede about art school, but Dede would not listen.

"What should I do?" Emily asked Dick one night.

"You could talk to Mr. Lawson," Dick suggested. "He is our legal guardian. He could give permission and make arrangements."

Emily thought about Dick's suggestion. The next week she walked into town to the lawyer's office. Mr. Lawson looked up at her from behind a huge dark wood desk. He had a wide loose face with bushy gray

eyebrows above round wire-rimmed eye-glasses and wild gray whiskers sprouting from his cheeks. He pushed down his glasses to look at her. His small eyes were shrewd but not unkind.

"What can I do for you, Emily?" he asked.

Emily had given the question of art school some thought. The best schools were in England and France, but these places were far away. There was a school in California, which was just two days to the south by boat.

"I would like to go away to study art," Emily told Mr. Lawson. "There is an art school in San Francisco. Could I go there, please?"

Mr. Lawson looked surprised.

"Have you talked to your sister about this?" he asked.

"She won't talk about it," Emily said.

Mr. Lawson frowned.

"Is this something you are serious about, Emily? You're sure it isn't just a passing whim?"

"Yes, very sure," Emily said, meeting his eyes.

He seemed to sense her determination, and he nodded.

"Very well. I'll see what I can do," he said. Then, he returned his glasses to their perch on his nose and looked down at the stack of papers on his desk. She was dismissed.

A few days later, Dede stopped Emily as she came in the front door. Her hands were on her hips, and her look was dark.

"So, you went behind my back, did you?" she said. She must have spoken with Mr. Lawson.

For a moment, Emily felt a twinge of guilt. Dede looked angry but also something else. Could Emily have hurt her feelings?

"I tried to talk to you about it," Emily explained, but her voice sounded defensive, angry, and she didn't want it to. She hadn't gone to Mr. Lawson to go behind Dede's back or to spite Dede; she'd done it because she loved art, and she wanted to go to art school.

Emily took a deep breath. She did not want to fight with Dede. She wanted Dede to understand.

"I want to be an artist," she said.

Dede sighed. Her eyes seemed to soften slightly.

"Very well," she said. "If you want to go to San Francisco to study art, you shall go."

Dede's mouth formed into a small thin smile. "And you shall stay with the Piddingtons, under their supervision," she added.

The Piddingtons! Emily had been so glad to be rid of them, she hadn't paid any attention to where she'd been told they were going. She'd completely forgotten they were staying in San Francisco.

Oh, well. It didn't matter. Once she was away from Dede's rule, she could do what she wanted. Not even the Piddingtons could dampen her joy. She was going to study art.

"I'm going to San Francisco!" Emily told Dick and Alice that night. She sprawled on her back on top of her bed, her arms spread wide.

"Oh Emily!" Alice was horrified. "That's such a big, wicked city."

"I'll be safe with the Piddingtons," Emily

said with a wry smile. She explained what Dede was arranging, and Dick couldn't help laughing. Alice shook her head, relieved.

"You and Dede are so much alike," she said.

Emily sat up. "No, we're not!" she said.

Alice laughed.

"For one thing, you're both stubborn," she said.

"And you both want to have the last word," Dick added as he plunked down on the foot of the bed

"You're both talented," Alice added.

Emily opened her mouth to object further, then closed it. It was true that their older sister was a talented artist in her own way—in the womanly arts of needlework and painting on china. But she had not chosen art as Emily had—or maybe it was more accurate to say art had not chosen her the way it had chosen Emily.

"And you love each other," Alice said, looking at Emily.

"Huh!" Emily scoffed. "She has a fine way of showing it."

"She's just trying to take care of us the best way she knows how," Alice said softly. "She worries about you ... We all do."

Emily rolled her eyes, but inside she was quiet. She was glad to be going away, but she was also a bit worried. And she would miss everyone. Dick too was silent— perhaps thinking about how he would feel when he was gone.

"Enough melodrama!" Emily announced suddenly, springing to her feet. She stepped over to the canary's cage and whistled. The canary cocked his head, and Emily whistled again. Then Emily cocked her head to one side to show she was waiting for his answer. Alice made an impatient sound.

"Shh," Emily whispered. "Listen ..."

A moment later, the little bird's song filled the room.

"See?" Emily said. "He agrees."

"About what?" Alice asked.

"About coming with me to California and about his name," Emily told them.

"What name?" Dick asked.

"I've decided to call him Dick, and whenever I hear him sing, I'll think of home."

Alice smiled and Dick grinned broadly.

Emily smiled with them. She'd have her bird to remind her of family, and she'd have the memory of rides with Johnny to keep the wild places close. And she'd be back.

Afterword

Emily Carr was born in Victoria, British Columbia in 1871, the same year British Columbia stopped being a colony of the British Empire and joined the Canadian Federation. In later years Emily wrote about her life as an artist, giving us glimpses of her Victoria childhood in *The Book of Small* (Irwin, 1942) and *Growing Pains: an Autobiography* (Irwin, 1946). From these small glimpses, I developed my fictional story to try to fill in the gaps and imagine what kind of girl Emily was and what it was like for her to struggle to follow her dream.

In *Growing Pains*, Emily says she was almost sixteen when she approached the family lawyer to ask if she could go away to art school. Records show that she was actually closer to nineteen when she left for San Francisco in 1890. In this book, I have stayed true to Emily's own memory of how old she was, even though it is not accurate, strictly speaking.

She studied art at the California School of Design in San Francisco for three years before returning to Victoria. Once at home again, Emily had the old cow barn loft converted into a studio where she taught art to local children. She also made her first visit to a First Nations village near Ucluelet on the west coast of Vancouver Island, where she was deeply moved by the people and their carvings.

Emily saved the money she earned from teaching art, storing it in a pair of old shoes tied from a rafter in the cow loft studio. When she had enough saved she went to England to study further. She also spent time in France studying art and learning a new style of painting that used color in a less realistic, more emotional way. On her return to Canada, she taught art in Victoria and Vancouver and saved money to travel up the British Columbia coast, visiting and painting First Nations villages and totem poles, as well as the surrounding forest. Eventually she focused her painting on the trees themselves, developing a unique style that captures the living spirit of the wild West Coast forests.

Being a female artist at a time when women were expected to be wives and mothers and nothing more, and painting in a new style that many people did not appreciate often made life difficult for Emily. Although her paintings were exhibited in well-known art galleries, and many important people praised Emily's work, Emily never felt totally accepted and understood. Yet, even in the face of disappointment and discouragement, she continued to stay true to her dream. Today, Emily Carr is one of Canada's best loved and best known artists.

When **Jacqueline Pearce** was a child, her grandmother lived right around the corner from Emily Carr's house. Jacqueline used to wish that she had a pair of magic glasses that would show her what Victoria was like when Emily Carr was young. Now she has created a pair of books that provide child readers with more than a glimpse. Jacqueline is the author of several other books, including *Discovering Emily* and *The Reunion*. She lives in Burnaby, British Columbia.